PAROLED

A Forbidden Love, You Choose Your Steam Factor series, Book 3

Daphne Dennis

NOTE: These books contain two endings to suit YOUR preferences.

Do you prefer a romance with just a little steam? Read straight through, but STOP when you get to the **!

Do you prefer it hot and steamy? Skip the — chapter and go straight to the ** at the end.

Both chapters will have the same name, so choose if you're milder -- or ready for the heat **!

Social Stamina – 1,2,3 Let's Go!

Titles to help look at things from other perspectives and strengthen your mindset.

The Great Ascension–1,2,3 Let's Go!

Titles to help you gain focus and climb the ladder of success!

How to Start – 1,2,3 Let's Go!

Titles to help you with step-by-step, must-have knowledge of the business world and personal experiences.

Top 10 Questions to Ask Before You…1,2,3 Let's Go!

Titles with must-have questions (and logic behind) for many of life's daily and major decisions.

Find our fiction below!

https://www.ttpublishinghouse.com/legendsreborn

https://www.ttpublishinghouse.com/7wishes

https://www.ttpublishinghouse.com/mallcadet

Social Media

Facebook: tlmpublishinghouse

Website: www.TTpublishinghouse.com

Want to Read for Free?

You may qualify for a spot on our Advance Reader Copy group.

Never heard of an ARC Group?

Simply put, it's a small group of people who are interested in a specific genre and are invited to read books before they're published.

Your feedback can help alter the storyline or even catch an elusive typo!

You're asked to provide an honest review when it is published, and that's it!

You read for free!

Go now to confirm your interest in the ARC Group!
https://www.ttpublishinghouse.com/joinTLMarc

Contents

*Note: ***indicates steamy/erotica****

The Meeting

Dixie couldn't stop the giddy grin from spreading over her face if she tried. The guard that was leading her out of her cell gave her an incredulous look.

"I swear, you're the weirdest inmate we've ever had," she said.

Dixie gave a small laugh. "Just admit you're going to miss me, Amanda," she winked at her, and Amanda shook her head.

"Certainly, going to miss the shower karaoke," Amanda replied sarcastically. Dixie knew how much everyone hated her shower performances. Was she crazy for feeling a little bittersweet about leaving this place? She didn't know. What she did know was that there was much more 'sweet' than 'bitter.' She couldn't wait to get out of here.

"Thanks, Amanda," Dixie said as the guard uncuffed her wrists. She walked slowly into the room where an officer stood in front of one of the tables. She took a seat, but the man continued to stand.

"My name is Peter Mullaney; I'm your parole officer."

Dixie looked up at the man that stood in front of her. He had thick dark hair that was lightly streaked with grey and a deep scowl on his face. He could be kind of handsome, she supposed; if he hadn't been frowning so hard, she was worried his features would permanently set that way.

"Well, don't look so excited about it," she drawled at him with a lazy smile.

"Miss Martinez,"

"Just Dixie's fine," she interrupted him.

"Miss Martinez," he repeated sharply, "as you know, you're being released on parole."

"Kinda hard to forget since the hearing was just yesterday."

"The conditions of your parole were already laid out to you, I believe," he continued like she hadn't spoken, "but you and I will be going over them again for clarity."

"Are you just going to stand there the whole time or are you going to take a seat?" she asked. They were in the prison visiting room, and they were the only ones there. Peter Mullaney was standing behind the empty seat opposite Dixie, his entire body tense like he was ready to fight at any second. Dixie didn't know whether not to laugh at how uncomfortable he seemed.

"Come on," she cajoled. "My neck's gonna start hurting if I have to look up at you this whole time."

After a few moments of him staring at her tensely, Officer Mullaney finally took a seat opposite her.

"There, see, that wasn't so hard, was it?" she asked cheekily. "Never seen a cop so uncomfortable around a criminal, though."

"I'm not uncomfortable," he ground out. "But you're right, you are a criminal."

The malice in his tone caught Dixie off guard, and she raised her hands in a mock surrendering posture. "Hey, you don't have to tell me twice; I'm the one in here. Not for too long anymore, though," she grinned, lowering her hands.

"Parole is a privilege, Miss Martinez," Officer Mullaney said. "It's not something to take lightly."

"I'm not taking anything lightly, so you can calm down with the accusations, okay?" she rolled her eyes.

They both fell silent, once again engaging in a silent staring contest of sorts.

"So, are we going to go over the conditions, or what?" she asked finally when he remained silent.

He pulled out some documents from the briefcase he was carrying. "These are your papers and the conditions of your parole." He set the papers on the table between them and slid one over to Dixie.

"First of all, you'll have to acquire and maintain both a residence and employment," he started. "You have two weeks to sort that out. I can assist with either of these if necessary, but I would prefer if you made your own plans."

Dixie gave a dry laugh. "Of course, you would."

He paused to glare at her before continuing. "You'll also be required to engage in weekly community service. The details of the service have already been determined and can be found in these documents," he pointed to a folder and went on. "You will refrain from the use of alcohol, drugs, or other substances for the duration of your parole. You will stay within the city limits for the duration of your parole. Your parole officer, which is me, is permitted to make surprise visits to your home or place of employment to ensure that you comply with these conditions."

"I can't believe you're making getting out of prison sound boring," Dixie said, cutting him off. "Must be a talent."

The officer put down the papers he was holding and took a deep breath. "Miss Martinez, do you think this is a joke?" he asked. His voice was calm, but she could hear his impatience in his tone.

"Peter, can I call you Peter?" she asked.

"No."

"Look, Peter, none of this is a joke to me," she said, ignoring his response. "But it is a great thing, and I don't need your dull tone and death glare trying to convince me otherwise."

"The guards around here have told me about you, you know?" he said, leaning back in his chair. "You like to laugh around the prison. Make friends. You like it in here, don't you?"

"I don't like it here," she snapped back at him. "But I'm flattered that you asked around about me." She batted her eyelashes at him and smiled mockingly. "That's a lot of effort for someone who doesn't want to be here."

"Don't flatter yourself," he rolled his eyes.

Dixie dropped her smile and rolled hers. "I don't understand why you're trying to make me into some sort of monster for trying to make the best of a bad situation."

Dixie knew that some of the other prisoners had found her weird for maintaining her optimism for her entire imprisonment. But she knew that it was the only way she would make it through. Every night in her cell, she had gone over the things she had done to get there, and she knew that if she could go back she wouldn't change anything. Parole had never been her plan. She was going to serve her full sentence and make the best of it while she was there. She counted down the days until she could see Sarah and Elliot again. When the option for parole came, it was a gift that she accepted wholeheartedly.

"A bad situation?" he laughed humourlessly. "You mean dealing with the consequences of your actions. I know what you're in here for. And you think this is just a 'bad situation.'"

"There's a lot you don't know or understand, so you better stop talking about things you don't have any idea about," Dixie replied.

He shook his head. "There's always some story or the other, isn't there?"

"Well, I must have done something right since we're sitting here right now."

He shook his head again. "You were lucky to get parole. And, from your track record, who knows how long that's going to last."

"Don't you think you're a bit out of line, basically telling me you want to see me fail?" she asked incredulously.

"Oh, this isn't about what I want," he said. "This is about the inevitable. Do you know how many people make it through their parole without getting sent back in? Once a criminal, always a criminal. So, maybe don't get too comfortable when you get out, okay?"

Peter's words stung. Dixie was used to the word 'criminal.' The guards used it all the time. She used it on herself too. The girls in prison sometimes joked about which of them was the worst of the bunch. But, in her heart, Dixie always believed that she was a good person. She knew what she had done, and that was why she willingly chose to serve her time. Despite her self-assurance, something about the way Peter called her a criminal stung. It felt like he cared less about what she had done or why she had done it and more about who she was as a person. Peter didn't see any good in her. He likely never would. Dixie knew that she would have to accept that if she wanted to stay sane during their meetings every week for the foreseeable future. Still, her stubborn nature pushed her to keep arguing.

"What do you have against me, man? You don't even know me!" Dixie threw her hands up in frustration.

"I don't have to," Peter said, leaning across the table to fix her with a hard, hate-filled glare. "I know your type. You think what you did wasn't so serious, and you want to act like you were just a victim of circumstance, but you're just like everyone else in here."

Dixie huffed out a breath at his words. "Makes sense that a cop would only see the world in black and white," she replied, leaning back. "You think I'm as bad as everyone else in here? Fine. But I'm getting out tomorrow, and I don't care how you feel about me; I am going to make this work with or without you."

"Trust me, I wish 'without' was an option."

"You're kind of awful at your job, you know that?" she asked as he packed up the documents on the table before them. "Probably hundreds of officers available, and I get stuck with you."

"As long as I keep sending your kind in here, I think I'm doing pretty okay at my job," he replied, not looking up from his briefcase. He stood up, gripping the case in his hands.

"Miss Martinez," he gave her a small nod and turned to walk away.

"Hey, Peter!" she called to him. He paused but didn't turn around as he waited to see what she would say. "If you've been sending people like me in here, you're even worse at your job than I thought."

Officer Mullaney didn't bother giving her a response as he strode out of the prison.

This is going to be a disaster, Dixie thought.

Homecoming

"**D**ixie!"

Dixie had barely made it out of the prison gates before her arms were full of her crying sister. Sarah had always been a crier. When they were younger, the tiniest things would set her off. Sometimes, Sarah would start crying because she thought someone was about to cry.

Dixie had always been the tougher of the two, but even she couldn't stop a tear or two from dropping. She squeezed her sister tight, knowing that Sarah would never judge her or make her feel weak for crying. Dixie didn't want to be cheesy, but she felt like she was breathing new air. She had kept it together as best she could for the last year, but prison had taken a toll on her. And she didn't know if she could ever be the woman she was before.

"Okay, okay," Sarah pulled back from their tight embrace, sniffling, "we should head home. Can't have a full-on breakdown outside the prison gates."

"I think this is a great place for a breakdown, actually," Dixie joked, and Sarah let out a wet laugh.

"Let's just get out of here." She grabbed her sisters' hands and intertwined their fingers. "If things go well, we'll never have to see this place again."

"Amen to that!"

The sisters held each other close as they made their way to Sarah's car. The drive to the city was quiet. Sarah turned the radio down, knowing that Dixie was prone to get lost in her thoughts. Dixie knew that she had a lot to think about-finding a job and a place to live being at the top of the list-but all she could do was stare out the window. Another cliché, but she was grateful to see trees again. To see other cars driving past them with people in them, living their lives. People thought that the worst thing about prison was the work or fighting. Gangs maybe. As far as Dixie was concerned, the worst thing about prison was the isolation. Having no idea how the rest of the world was doing out there. She spent a year without any access to the media, entertainment, or anything from the outside world. And that had been what threatened to break her the most.

"Get your head out of the clouds, Dixie." Sarah's voice cut through Dixie's reflections, and she tore her gaze away from the window to look at her sister. Sarah gave her a dazzling smile. "We're home."

Sarah pulled her car into her small driveway, and Dixie felt her giddy excitement returning. She was a twenty-eight-year-old woman. There was no reason for her to be jumping in her seat at the thought of a home-cooked dinner. But Dixie had to admit that she was.

"Oh, God, please tell me you have something ready to eat," she groaned as she got out of the car. "And where's the little monster?" just as she asked the question, a tiny blur of a person dashed out of the house, launching themselves into Dixie's arms.

"Aunt Dixie!" the young boy shouted.

"You are just like your mom!" Dixie laughed, wrapping her arms around him. "Y'all don't even give me a second to catch my breath."

"I missed you, Aunt Dixie," he said, tightening his small arms around her.

"I missed you too, Elliot," she said, returning his embrace. "Let me get a look at you," she held him at arm's length, making a show of scrutinizing him from head to toe. "You're so big now!" she said with an exaggerated face. "How old are you, a hundred?"

"I'm just seven, silly," he giggled, preening under the praise.

"Just seven, and you're already so big and strong?" Dixie asked, laying it on thick. "By the time you're eight, you're going to be towering over all of us."

Elliot took her hand and started to pull her in. "I have so much to show you, Aunt Dixie," he babbled as he led her into the house. "I've got a bunch of new toys, and I got an award in class, and mommy got a new TV, so I have so many games!"

Dixie laughed as she let the boy pull her into the house. Elliot had always shared the same eager enthusiasm towards life that she did. She and Sarah joked about it a lot. Sarah was the calm one that always knew how to temper her emotions and see the bigger picture, while Dixie rushed into things and thought with her heart instead of her head. Somehow, Elliot had completely taken after Dixie, always talking a mile a minute and letting his emotions lead his way. It was the thing Dixie loved the most about the kid. Where their parents had made Dixie feel awful her entire childhood for being too loud and playful, she was determined to show Elliot that there was nothing wrong with the way they were. In many ways, Sarah having a kid had been the best thing to happen to Dixie. Elliot's birth had brought the sisters closer in a way that they had never been growing up. Their relationship had only grown stronger still when Elliot's father had abandoned him and Sarah, prompting Dixie to step up as the big sister.

She remembered the night that Sarah had called her crying that Jason had left them. She remembered the fierce rush of protectiveness she had felt as she held Sarah and baby

Elliot in a tight embrace as Sarah sobbed uncontrollably. She had sworn in that very moment, all those years ago, that she would do anything for the two of them. And she would always keep that promise.

She humored Elliot for a while as he showed her around the house and all the new things that they had gotten since she left. While Sarah had visited her multiple times while she was in prison, Dixie had always insisted that Elliot not come. Shame wasn't an emotion that she felt often, but she knew that she wouldn't be able to handle her time in the prison if Sarah ever had to bring Elliot in there. One of the few possessions she had been allowed to keep in her cell was a small picture of the three of them taken from Elliot's first trip to the fair. That picture had been her north star throughout the last year.

"Okay, baby, let Aunt Dixie get settled in and get some dinner, okay?" Sarah said to Elliot after about an hour of him explaining his latest game obsession to Dixie. She couldn't claim that she understood half of what he was saying, but seeing him so happy put a smile on her face.

"But mom…" Elliot whined.

"None of that, honey," Sarah scolded. "Don't you have some homework to do?"

Elliot reluctantly got to his feet and headed to his room. Once he was gone, Sarah led Dixie to the table. "Here you go," she said, placing a steaming dish piled with rice and chicken in front of her.

Dixie groaned as the scent hit her nose. She grabbed a fork and dug in before Sarah was even done setting the dish down, causing her sister to laugh at her. Dixie groaned again at the taste. "God, I missed your food so much! This is amazing, thank you."

"No thanks needed," Sarah said, sitting opposite her with a dish of her own. The sisters ate in silence for some minutes, both focusing on enjoying their meals before Sarah finally spoke up.

"So, what's the plan now?" she asked.

Dixie gulped water to push down her food before answering.

"Well, I have to find a job and a place to live," she said. "I know it's a bit of a bother, but I was hoping I could stay here for a while."

"Are you kidding, Dix?" Sarah asked. "Of course, you're staying here. You really thought I'd let you live somewhere alone?"

"I don't want to impose on you and Elliot," Dixie started.

"Elliot loves you," Sarah said firmly. "And we owe you everything."

"Come on, Sarah," Dixie said, shaking her head. "You don't owe me anything. We're family."

"Not all family would do what you did for us, Dixie. And I will never be able to repay you for it," Sarah said soberly.

Dixie reached out and took her sister's hand in hers. "There's nothing to repay, okay? Let's not talk about it anymore. I did what I did, and I'd do it a hundred times over."

Sarah looked like she still had so much more to say, but she left it all unsaid. "Fine, but you are staying here. We'll work on getting you a job tomorrow. I'm sure places are hiring around town. We can look around for something part-time for now."

"Alright," Dixie nodded. She let go of her sister's hand and turned back to her food.

"I'm going to check on Elliot," Sarah said, getting up. "The guest room is already set up for you. Get some rest, okay?"

Dixie nodded, and Sarah leaned over to kiss her forehead as she walked out.

Dixie looked down at her food, feeling tears well up in her eyes. She was home again, finally.

***

"This is the third time this week I've had to prevent you from getting arrested, Joshua." Peter slammed the door behind him as he followed his son into their home. Joshua had his head hung low, but Peter knew that it wasn't with remorse. He didn't know how to get through to Joshua anymore. The boy just wasn't listening.

"Talk to me, Josh," he pleaded as his son headed to the kitchen. "Are you acting out over something? Is it those guys you've been hanging out with that have you doing all these crazy things?"

"It's nothing, dad!" Joshua burst out. "I'm not acting out; I'm just. Hanging out. I didn't mean to get in trouble; I'm sorry."

"I don't need an apology, Josh; I need an explanation," Peter replied, exasperated.

"Well, I don't have one for you, okay?" Joshua replied. "Why don't you just butt out and focus on your job or whatever."

"Is that what this is about?" Peter asked. "You think I've been working too much? Cause I've barely been active since I got out of the hospital, but I can talk to my chief about reducing my hours if that's what you want."

"I don't want anything, dad; everything isn't about you!" Joshua screamed before storming out of the kitchen and heading to his room. He slammed the door behind him, and the echo resounded through their small space.

Pater sat heavily at the dining table and put his head in his hands. He didn't know what to do about Joshua anymore. Claudia would have known what to do. She was always so good at handling Joshua. Could this be a delayed reaction to Claudia's death? Peter didn't know where to start forming his theories on Joshua's behavior. All he knew was that he had to do something about it quickly before his son ended up like his late wife.

Joshua had been caught earlier that day with a group of neighborhood delinquents. They had been drinking and gambling, both of which were illegal activities, as Josh was only seventeen years old. Peter thought he had done his best since Claudia died four years ago, but lately, he was feeling more and more like he was losing his grip on his son.

His phone beeped with a reminder. He had his first parole meeting with Dixie Martinez tomorrow. He groaned at the reminder. He knew that doing parole duty was the best work he could get at the moment. He had been shot a few months ago while trying to apprehend a grocery store thief, and he couldn't return to active duty for the time being. Luckily, he was also registered as a parole officer, so he could continue working.

Something about Dixie Martinez rubbed him the wrong way. He usually did his best to regulate his emotions and biases around people. He had become a police officer because of his deep disdain for any sort of crime. He could never understand why someone would choose to turn to crime, no matter what their circumstances were. His own father had been a lowlife drug and weapons dealer, and he had seen first-hand how dealing in illegal activities left a person's life in shambles. So, he rarely had any sympathy for people who chose to walk down those paths. If they wanted to do illegal things, they had better be ready to deal with the consequences of their choices.

Dixie Martinez acted like she was having the time of her life, even while she was serving a two-year sentence for theft. Peter had read her file before accepting to be her parole officer. She had robbed four jewelry stores, disabling their security systems and breaking in before she finally got caught. There was no excuse for that kind of crime.

Peter dreaded seeing her the next day, but he was determined not to let her rile him up. He had lost his cool at the prison a few weeks ago, but he could handle being her parole officer. She had already reported to him that she had found a job and a place to live, so Peter was relieved that he didn't have to handle that for her. He only had to deal with seeing her once a week. If he was lucky, he would get replaced in a few months when he was fit for duty again, and he could get back to catching criminals instead of getting lunch with them and pretending like they had changed just because they behaved well in prison.

With a deep sigh, he got to his feet and headed to bed. He had a lot on his plate, and he needed some rest.

First Session

"Hey there, Pete". Dixie greeted. "Looking pleasant as always."

Peter was sitting at one of the lunch tables in the soup kitchen cafeteria. Her weekly community service included a shift at the soup kitchen, and Peter had suggested that they have their parole meetings there so she could kill two birds with one stone. He was as handsome as last time, but Dixie was determined not to pay any attention to that, because he was also scowling as hard as last time.

She had still been working behind the counter when he arrived, so he had waited for her at a table. Now that she was done, she dropped a tray in front of him that was piled with the lasagne she had helped make earlier that day.

"Hope you're hungry," she said, grinning.

"It's Officer Mullaney," he said, pushing the tray back a few inches, "and no, I'm not, thank you."

Dixie gave a good-natured shrug and pulled his tray closer to hers. "More for me then."

She dug into her own plate of lasagne and watched as Peter barely held back his look of disgust. She felt smugly validated at the fact that she affected him so much.

"Let's make this quick," he said.

"Isn't there like, a minimum time that our meetings are supposed to last?" Dixie asked, mouth half full.

"No," he replied shortly. "There isn't."

"Alright, let's get this over with then."

Peter pulled out some documents and looked up at Dixie.

"Are you going to stop eating and pay attention?" he asked impatiently.

"You have my full attention; just tell me what you need."

He rolled his eyes. "I need proof that you have a job and proof of residence."

Dixie dug out a folder from her bag and handed it to Peter. "I have my employment letter in there and proof of residence."

"How were you able to find a job and a house on such short notice?" he asked suspiciously.

"You're a very distrustful man, do you know that?" she asked rhetorically. "I guess that comes in handy, being a cop and all. What's your dating life like? I bet women love the whole brooding thing."

"Miss Martinez," Peter said tersely.

"I was just trying to make conversation!" she said, shrugging innocently. "I'm living with my sister, okay? And she helped me get a job too. Check it out," she gestured to the folder. Peter opened it up and pulled out her employment letter.

"You're a cashier at a grocery store," he said blandly. "Are you sure you'll be able to control yourself around the register? Sticky fingers and all."

"You are *so* unprofessional," Dixie laughed. "That was a good one, though."

Peter gave her an incredulous look. "That wasn't a joke," he said.

"But it was funny," she replied.

"How are you so nonchalant about everything?" he asked.

"How are you so boring all the time?" she countered.

Peter gave out a frustrated huff.

"Look, I know you think I'm a good-for-nothing criminal. And I'm not going to sit here and try to convince you to care about me. But we are stuck with each other, so why don't we just try to be civil? What do you say?"

She held out a hand expectantly. Peter eyes her outstretched hand for a few moments before begrudgingly placing his hand in hers.

"We'll be civil."

***

"You're looking excited for someone who's heading to community service," Sarah commented. It had been a few weeks of Dixie settling into a routine of working part-time at the grocery store, doing her community service, attending her court-mandated therapy, and meeting with Peter weekly. She didn't want to sound too optimistic, but she thought she was starting to wear him down. His comments didn't have the bite of hatred that they once did, and she had even caught him almost laughing at her jokes a few times.

Dixie shrugged at her sister. "Just happy to be free and alive," she replied.

"And this doesn't have anything to do with a certain attractive police officer?" she asked.

"Oh, my God, Sarah!" Dixie exclaimed. "It's not like that between us. He hates me."

"It didn't look like he hated you last week when I came to pick you up from the soup kitchen, and you two were staring into each other's eyes," Sarah replied slyly.

"We were having a staring contest!" Dixie protested.

"Is that how older people flirt now? How subtle."

"Shut up!" she exclaimed. "I'm going to therapy first today, okay? I'll be back after meeting with Peter."

"Want me to come and pick you up?" Sarah asked.

"Nah, I'll just take the bus."

"Or you could ask Peter to drop you off," Sarah said with a wink.

"Bye, Sarah," Dixie said, shaking her head at her sister's antics.

The court-mandated therapy had been a recent addition to her parole conditions, and this was only her second session, but she liked her therapist, Sheila Cross. She was very professional and caring, and she let Dixie talk about whatever she wanted. Dixie doubted that she would ever want to talk about why she went to prison, but she was happy to discuss soap operas and Elliot's grade school drama with Dr. Cross.

The therapy went well. The most exciting thing that happened was meeting a man who appeared to be Dr. Cross's boyfriend. His name was Mark, and Dixie had been surprised to see the usually put-together therapist blush when asked about him.

"It's only been a few months," Sheila had said. "We're still figuring out a lot of things."

Dixie was happy for the woman. She didn't know her well yet, but Dixie could tell that Sheila was the kind of woman that needed more love in her life.

After the therapy session and her shift at the soup kitchen, Dixie found herself excited for her parole meeting. She shoved aside the feeling, blaming Sarah for putting those thoughts in her head. There would never be anything like that between her and Peter. He was too rigid for her. And besides, wasn't it illegal to date your parole officer?

She forced herself to think of something else as Peter arrived. He approached her at their usual table and surveyed the trays she had set before them.

"Today's special!" she announced in and showy voice as he approached. "Gourmet mac and cheese!" she gestured to the trays in front of her and smiled to herself as Peter just barely held back a smile at her performance. "What will our judge make of today's meal?"

"Nice try," Peter said, taking a seat, "but you're not going to make me eat anything here."

"It was worth a try," Dixie shrugged. This was something else that had become a routine. She would set out two trays of food for them and try to convince Peter to eat with her. He always refused, letting her have both trays. Dixie had always been a good eater, but since returning from prison, she had been eating more than ever. She blamed her quick metabolism and a year of barely eating prison food for why her appetite was so huge. Either way, she enjoyed her little game with Peter and was happy to eat both meals.

"You went to therapy this morning, right?" he asked.

Dixie nodded in response, not wanting to talk with her mouth full. A few weeks ago, she would have done so just to annoy Peter. But he had surprisingly honored their agreement to be civil, reducing the number of jabs he threw at her, so she tried not to antagonize him too much.

"How was it?" he asked. "You like Dr. Cross?"

Dixie shrugged and swallowed down the food in her mouth. "She's nice. I don't really know why I needed therapy, though."

"The board suggested it," Peter said, sounding tired after explaining this to Dixie about three times before now. "They thought it would be helpful for you to talk about what led you to... you know. Everything."

"There's nothing to talk about," Dixie said lightly. "I did what I did, and that's it."

"Dixie," Peter said her name in a stern tone, and Dixie looked up. It had taken him weeks to finally stop calling her Miss Martinez, and it was still a pleasant surprise every time he said her name.

"You must have done what you did for a reason," he said. "I can't imagine what that reason is, and I can't condone it, but talking about it just might help."

"I've told you there's nothing to talk about," Dixie snapped. "Can we drop this, or do you want to play therapist some more."

Peter sighed in frustration. "I'm reaching out here, Dixie," he said.

"I don't need you to," she replied shortly. "You've already made it abundantly clear how you feel about me, and I'm fine with that. If I want to pour my heart out, I'll do it with the shrink, alright?"

Dixie was surprised to see a hurt expression on Peter's face before he schooled his features to passivity.

"Fine."

He got to his feet. "I think we're done for this week," he said.

"Sounds good to me."

They cleaned up the table in uncomfortable silence.

"Is Sarah coming to get you?" he asked as they approached the exit.

"I'm taking the bus," she replied as he opened the doors.

The sound and sight of pouring rain greeted them. Peter and Dixie glanced at each other at the same time.

"You can't go out in this," he said, gesturing to the rain. "Let me take you home."

"It's fine; I can make it," Dixie said, squaring her shoulders.

"Don't be stupid, Dixie," he said with a sigh. "Come on; we can make a run for my car."

He used his jacket as a shield from the rain above him, and Dixie did the same. They ran out into the downpour, getting soaked in seconds. Dixie threw herself into the passenger seat of Peter's car, shivering as he got into the driver's seat. He started up the car and turned on the heat, and she rubbed her arms to try and generate some warmth.

"Still think you could have made it to the bus station?" Peter asked.

"Oh, shut up," Dixie replied good-naturedly, causing both of them to burst into laughter.

He headed out when they had both caught their breath and started making his way down the street.

"You remember where Sarah's house is?" she asked. He had come over once to verify that her address was legitimate, and it had been a hilarious encounter between him and Elliot. Elliot had tried to intimidate Peter, wary of cops since Dixie had gotten arrested, and Peter had to pretend like Elliot posed a real threat to him.

"Of course I do; what kind of cop do you think I am?" he asked with faux outrage.

"I thought we already established that you weren't the best at the job," Dixie joked.

Peter glanced at her at those words, and she froze, wondering if she had hit a nerve. She had made that jab at him before they knew anything about each other, and he had prided himself on putting 'people like her' in prison. Did he still feel the same way?

"Well, you might be on to something," Peter said finally, leaving Dixie to try and decrypt what he meant by that as his phone began to ring.

"This is Mullaney," Peter answered his phone. He slammed on the brakes, sending Dixie forward. Her seatbelt holding her back, but the force of the stop knocked the breath out of her.

"Where?" Peter demanded. He was quiet for a second as whoever he was speaking to responded. "I'm on my way." He tossed his phone aside and started driving, face tight with concentration.

"Is everything okay?" Dixie asked.

"My son, Joshua," Peter said, voice tight. "He's in the hospital?"

"What happened?"

"They said he overdosed. I don't know... I don't know, Dixie," Peter's voice broke as he said her name, and Dixie reached out a hand and rested it on his shoulder.

"It'll be okay," she said, trying to sound reassuring. "Let's go and see what exactly is going on, okay?"

"I, I have to take you home first," Peter stammered.

"No way," Dixie shook her head. "Hospital first, okay."

Peter gave a slight nod, and they drove to the hospital in silence.

They rushed through the hospital hallways in a daze as Peter identified himself and was led to the doctor's office. Dixie waited in the hall as Peter talked to the doctors. A nurse gave her a blanket when they noticed she was shivering. Dixie didn't even register the cold. She was too worried about Peter and his son. Peter hadn't talked about Joshua a lot, but she knew that Joshua was his everything.

After some time, Peter came out of the office looking shell-shocked.

Dixie rose to her feet and approached him. "What happened? Is he okay?"

Peter collapsed onto a chair and put his head in his hands.

"He had an overdose," he said. "Different drugs, all kinds of crap in him. They found him alone in an alley. The guys he was messing around with called an ambulance and bolted before they could get caught. I don't know where I went wrong with him."

"Hey," she said, pulling his hands from his face. "This isn't your fault, okay? Sometimes kids just act out, no matter how hard their parents try. Is he going to be okay?"

"He had to have some sort of emergency surgery. He's still in surgery now."

"How long till he gets out?"

"A few hours, the doctor said."

"Alright." Dixie got to her feet. "Do you want anything from the vending machine? Some tea or coffee?"

Peter looked up at her in confusion. "You should go home."

"Do you have anyone to stay here with you? Joshua's mom?"

Peter shook his head. "She died a few years ago. It's just him and me."

"Then I'm not leaving you here alone," she said firmly. "So, tea or coffee?"

Peter gave her an unreadable expression. She didn't bother trying to decipher it.

"Coffee," he said finally.

***

"Are you sure you don't want to go home?" Peter asked. The hospital hallway was mostly deserted, and they were both wrapped up in blankets, curled up on couches in the waiting room. Dixie checked her phone for the time. It was nearly midnight. Joshua had come out of surgery a few hours ago, but Peter wouldn't be allowed to see him till morning.

"I told you I'm not leaving you alone," she replied around a huge yawn. "We should probably get some sleep, though."

Peter fell silent, and Dixie snuggled into herself on the couch, shutting her eyes. She had already texted Sarah to tell her that she wouldn't be coming home that night.

"Why are you here?"

Peter's voice was so quiet that she wouldn't have heard it if the room wasn't already completely silent.

She sat up and faced him. "Look, I know you don't always think the best of me. But I'm not just going to leave you to deal with something like this alone."

"You're nothing like I thought you would be," Peter said.

"People rarely are."

"Why did you do it?"

"I just said-"

"The stealing, Dixie," he interrupted her. "It just doesn't make sense. You're not a bad person. No one commits multiple crimes and willingly goes to prison. I heard you even turned yourself in."

"Just drop it, Peter," she said, turning back and covering herself with her blanket.

"I can't," he said. "You contradict yourself at every turn, and it's driving me crazy. So, what's the truth?"

Dixie sat up again and pushed her blanket off her shoulders. "You want to know the truth?" she asked. "Fine." She took a deep breath. "I didn't commit any of those thefts. My sister did."

"What?" Peter asked. His mouth was slightly agape.

"Sarah's ex-boyfriend... my nephew's dad. He was the worst type of guy. Sarah was head over heels. She just fell so hard. I still don't understand it. He ditched them a few months after Elliot was born. I thought it was good riddance. But then he showed up again a year ago. He charmed Sarah all over again. She and I fought so badly over it that we didn't talk for months. That was when he convinced her to do the robberies. He had planned for her to take the fall. He planted all this evidence that led back to her. I couldn't let her go to prison. Not when she had Elliot to take care of. So, I took the fall for her. And I'd do it again, every single time."

Peter looked speechless at her admission. When he remained silent, Dixie wrapped her blanket around herself and prepared to lay back.

"What about the boyfriend? Why didn't you turn him in?" he asked.

"He was long gone, and I didn't want to bring him back into Sarah's life," Dixie shrugged. "Besides, if I turned him in, he would have implicated Sarah as well. Which kinda defeats the entire purpose of trying to protect her."

Peter shook his head and looked at her in wonder. "You're an idiot; you know that?"

Dixie chuckled lightly. "Believe it or not, you're not the first person to tell me that."

She lay back down on the couch and listened as Peter did the same.

"What you did for your sister was amazing," he said in the silence. "You're a great sister."

"Thank you."

The Visitor

"My name is Dixie Martinez; I'm here to see Joshua Mullaney."

"What are you doing here?"

Dixie looked away from the receptionist as Peter approached her from down the hallway.

"I wanted to see how Joshua was doing," she said, shrugging.

"I already told you he was doing fine," Peter replied.

"Well, maybe I wanted to meet the little rascal," she countered. "And check up on you as well," she added.

It had been two days since the night they spent in the hospital where Dixie had told him the truth, and they had barely talked since then. It wasn't as if they usually kept in constant contact- they exchanged a few texts here and there about parole meetings and such- but Dixie had felt different since that night. She had texted Peter to ask how Joshua was doing and when he replied with a simple 'fine,' she decided to come and check for herself.

"I'm fine," Peter said, giving her a small smile. "If you really want to meet Joshua, though, he's awake right now." He looked down at his feet and back up at her, and Dixie realized that he was nervous. Maybe things had changed for him, too, after all.

"I'd love to meet him," Dixie replied. "Lead the way."

Peter grinned at her and led her down the hallway to Joshua's room.

"He's been in an awful mood every time he's awake, but the doctors said he's going to be okay. He's only going to be in here for about a week or two," Peter explained as they stopped outside the door. "I'm sorry if he's rude or anything."

"Don't worry about me; I can deal with rude teenagers," Dixie said.

Peter gave her a grateful smile and opened the door. Joshua was the spitting image of his father. He had the same dark hair as Peter and the same sharp jaw. He was hooked up to an IV bag and had dark circles under his eyes.

"Hey, Joshua," Dixie greeted as she stepped in.

"Who is this?" Joshua asked his dad.

"This is Dixie; she's my…." Peter floundered for what word to use.

"Friend," Dixie filled in for him. "Your dad is usually my parole officer, but I'm here today as a friend."

"You're on parole?" Joshua asked. "Like, from prison?"

"That's right," Dixie nodded, taking another step into the room. Peter stayed at the door, watching them both. "I did some bad things and got locked up, but I have a chance to be free again now."

"I know what parole is; you don't have to explain it to me like I'm a kid," Joshua said haughtily.

"Well, if you didn't ask like a kid, I wouldn't have explained like a kid," Dixie retorted.

"Dixie!" Peter said, but before he could berate her for her tone, Joshua laughed loudly.

"I like her," he said to his dad.

"You're alright," she said, winking at Joshua, prompting him to laugh again. Peter looked like he was about to say something, but his phone rang. He glanced down at it and then back at the two of them.

"I should take this," he said hesitantly.

"We're good here," Dixie said. "Go on."

Peter looked like he was hesitating, but when his phone continued to ring, he stepped out to answer it.

"So," Joshua said as Dixie took the chair beside his bed. "Are you and my dad dating or something?"

Dixie let out a loud laugh at that. "Even if your dad wanted to date, he wouldn't dream of it cause he spends all his time worrying about you." Joshua's teasing expression fell to reveal a solemn one at her words. "Wanna tell me what happened here?" she asked.

"Why? You're just going to tell my dad anyway," he said stubbornly.

Dixie sighed and sank into her chair. "When I was fifteen, I almost got arrested for selling drugs. I didn't even need the money. I just wanted to get my parent's attention. Last year, I did something really stupid and ended up in prison. I know all about making bad decisions, kid. And I understand not wanting to see your parents' disappointment more than you'd think. So, if you don't want your dad to know what happened, he won't hear it from me. But if you want to talk about it, now's your chance."

Joshua looked surprised by her admission. She didn't say anything else as she let her words sink in for him. After a few moments of silence, Joshua cleared his throat.

"We were just messing around, me and the guys," he said. "They told me nothing would happen. Dared me to try some pills."

"Why were you hanging out with guys like that anyway?" Dixie asked, trying to sound as non-judgmental as possible.

"I don't know," Joshua said with a frustrated growl. "They're cool? They keep teasing me about being a cops kid, and I just wanted to prove that I could be cool too."

"Is that why you've been getting in trouble?" she asked. "You wanted to fit in with the cool kids?"

"It sounds dumb when you say it like that," he grumbled.

"No, it doesn't," Dixie assured him. "Hell, if anyone can relate to wanting to fit in with the cool crowd, it's me. I got into so much trouble when I was your age. My parents were the worst, you know? They never paid any attention to me. I thought hanging around the cool kids would make me important. If not to my parents, then to everyone else. But, you find out soon enough that people like that, they don't give a shit about you. See how they all abandoned you when you overdosed? They're not worth your time, Joshua."

He looked pensive as he thought over her words. "My dad is so mad at me," he said. "I've been giving him so much grief."

"Your dad loves you," Dixie said. "He's not going to care about anything else if you're in danger. You just have to do better and show him that you care too. Those guys you were hanging out with, they'll always leave when you need them. Your dad is always going to be there. Talk to him, okay?"

Joshua gave a small nod. "Yeah, okay," he said quietly.

"Don't make it too easy for him, though," Dixie said. "Your dad can be a bit of an asshole sometimes. Make him sweat for me, yeah?"

Joshua laughed loudly at Dixie's request, and Peter came back at that moment.

"You two look like you're getting along well," he said suspiciously.

"I was just boring Josh over here with stories of my childhood," Dixie said, getting to her feet. "But I should get going. Have a shift at work. See you tomorrow, Peter?" she asked.

"Tomorrow?" he asked, eyebrows scrunching in confusion.

"Our parole meeting?" she asked, grinning at his adorable confusion. "You know, the ones we have every Thursday?"

"Oh, right," Peter said, realization dawning. "I'm not sure if I'm going to be able to make it tomorrow," he said. "We can reschedule?"

"If you're going to be here, I could just come over again," she suggested. "Get some quality time with Joshua."

"I'd like that," Joshua piped up.

"I..." Peter looked between the two of them again. "Alright," he said.

"Sweet," Joshua said.

"See you both tomorrow, then," she said, leaning over to give Joshua a fist bump before leaving. She had a skip in her step as she left. Something had changed between her and Peter, and she didn't know whether she should chase it down or ignore it. All she knew was that Peter was looking at her differently, and for once, she didn't want to hold herself back from admiring him.

Over the next few days, she visited the hospital a lot. It turned out that Joshua and her had very similar senses of humor. That turned out to be a nightmare for Peter as they often joined forces to tease him. Her hospital visits often ended with the three of them hunched over in laughter and Dixie heading back home with a smile on her face.

"So, you're getting discharged tomorrow," Dixie said to Joshua. "Guess that's goodbye for us." She glanced at Peter as she spoke.

"No!" Joshua said. "You can come over to our place and hang out, can't you? Can't she, dad?" he asked, turning to Peter.

Peter glanced at Dixie before turning to his son. "It's not exactly that easy, son," he started.

"Come on, dad," he protested. "Dixie is my friend now. She should be able to come over sometimes. We have plans to game together!"

Peter shot her a questioning look, and she just shrugged. "I can't cancel the plans now," she said innocently.

"Fine, alright," Peter said with an exaggerated sigh. "Dixie can come over on weekends only, and only when she wants to, not when you do."

"Yes!" Joshua said, pumping his fist. "I can't wait to destroy you at Call of Duty."

"We'll see about that, punk," Dixie said, ruffling his hair. "I do have to get going, though."

"I'll walk you out," Peter said, getting up as well.

They walked down the hallway in cordial silence, arms brushing against each other. Sarah had lent Dixie the car that day, so they stopped beside it. It was early evening, and the sun was just starting to set. Dixie leaned back against the driver's door, and Peter stood in front of her with his hands in the pocket of his jacket.

"Thank you," he said, smiling down at her.

"What for?" she asked.

"Joshua." He shrugged. "Spending time with you has been good for him. I don't know what you said to him, but he's been more…open. So, thank you."

"You flatter me, officer," Dixie said coyly. "Who says I'm the reason he's been so open."

"I know it's you," Peter replied, not playing back to her teasing. "You're good at bringing out the best in people."

His honest words made Dixie pause. Peter was looking at her in a way he never had before. His eyes were filled with that unidentifiable emotion again. Dixie was tired of controlling herself around him. Without a second thought, she surged forward and planted her lips on his. Peter responded instantly like he had been waiting for her to kiss him.

They kissed passionately as Peter pulled her closer by the waist, and Dixie threw her arms around his neck. He leaned in pressing her against her car and leaning over her. Dixie ran her hands through his thick hair, and Peter shivered against her and pulled back.

"That wasn't… I didn't mean to," he stammered.

"I did," Dixie said. "I'll see you tomorrow, okay?"

"Yeah," he replied dumbly. Dixie couldn't help herself. She rose up on her toes and gave him one last quick kiss before getting in her car. As she drove off, she saw Peter still standing in the hospital parking lot, watching her drive away.

---The End? ---

"Aunt Dixie, you look pretty!" Elliot exclaimed. Dixie was brushing her hair in front of the mirror. She blushed slightly at the knowing look that Sarah gave her.

"I'm just going for a parole meeting, Elly," she said.

"What's a parole meeting?" Elliot asked.

"She's going to meet with Officer Peter," Sarah explained. "Remember him?"

Elliot nodded. "Is he your boyfriend, Aunt Dixie?"

"No!" Dixie replied, blushing harder.

"They're going on a date, though," Sarah said.

"No, we're not," Dixie corrected her.

"Oh, sorry, a 'parole meeting,' right?" Sarah asked, making air quotes around the words.

"I'm going to be late," Dixie mumbled. She grabbed her bag and the keys and headed out. It had been a week since Joshua had been released from the hospital, and she and Peter had shared that kiss. Dixie tried to push down the worry she felt, but they hadn't really talked since that day. He had missed their last parole meeting but suggested that they reschedule. When he suggested that they meet at a small diner that wasn't too far from her place, her hopes had risen again.

She was a jumbled mess of anticipation and nerves as she drove to the diner. She was a few minutes late, but she was surprised to see that Peter wasn't there when she arrived. She texted him as she got into a booth.

Hey, I'm at the diner. Are we still meeting?

It took a few minutes, but his reply eventually came.

I'm sorry I don't want to cancel again; we need to talk.

Dixie felt dread creep down her back. No one ever wanted to hear or see the words 'we need to talk' from the person they liked.

What about? She texted back.

We should do it in person. Do you think you could come over?

To your place? She asked, confused.

Yes.

His next message was an address.

Dixie sighed and got to her feet. She couldn't believe she was about to drive herself to go get dumped.

***

Peter's palms were sweating with nerves as he went to see the chief of the department. Thompson was known to be a hard-ass, but she had a soft spot for *family*. He had practiced his words countless times, so he knew he was prepared.

Her door opened, and he stepped in.

"What do you need, Mullaney?" she asked.

"I wanted to ask if I could be removed from parole duty," he said.

She looked up from the documents that she was holding. "Why?" she asked. "Parolee giving you problems?"

"No, nothing like that," he shook his head. "I just. My son just got out of the hospital. And I wanted to spend more time with him since I'm not back on active duty yet. I thought this would be the best opportunity."

Thompson looked at him with a scrutinizing gaze. "You sure about that, Mullaney?" she asked. "You're the one who asked to be put on parole."

"Yeah, I know," he said. "I just don't want to lose this opportunity to spend time with my son."

She gave him that scrutinizing look again before finally looking down. "Fine," she said. "You have a month. When you return, you're back on active duty."

"Thank you, chief," he said, sagging in relief.

"Yeah, yeah," she said, waving a hand at him. "Just make the most of it."

"Yes, ma'am," he said. He was already texting Dixie as he walked out of Thompson's office. He was going to get the girl. He drove home as fast as he could without breaking the speed limit. Dixie hadn't arrived by the time he got home, so he took a quick shower and ordered some food. When he heard a knock on the door, he knew it was her.

"Before you say anything, I just want you to know that you don't get to break up with me before we even started dating, okay?" Dixie barged in before he could say a word. "So, if you have some big break-up speech planned, you can save it."

She crossed her arms and glared at him, but he could see the vulnerability in her eyes.

"You think I asked you over here to dump you?" he asked, feeling a small grin begin to grow on his face.

"Why else would you say 'we need to talk'?" she asked.

"Maybe because I actually wanted to talk to you?" he said with a 'duh' tone.

"Talk, then," she challenged.

He couldn't hold the smile back now. "You are the most stubborn woman I know," he said, walking up to her. "You annoy the hell out of me, and you don't think before you act. You're brave and brash and so overwhelming sometimes."

"Kinda hard to tell if you're insulting or complimenting me, officer," she mumbled.

He stopped in front of her and held her face in his hands. "I'm in love with you, Dixie. I talked to my chief. I don't want to be your parole officer anymore. I want to be with you." Dixie looked up at him in disbelief. "Oh, now you're quiet?" he asked with a laugh.

She launched herself into his arms, sealing their lips together. If their first kiss had been a fire, this one was an inferno. They grabbed at each other's clothes as they stumbled across the room.

"Bedroom," Dixie panted against Peter's lips. "Please, Peter."

Peter nodded and led them to the bedroom without separating their lips. They crashed through the room and tumbled onto the bed together, giggling into each other's mouths.

"I'm in love with you too," Dixie whispered against his lips. "I want to be with you too."

Peter leaned down and took her lips again. His hands pushed her dress down her body, as Dixie nearly ripped his clothes off. When they were fully naked, she wrapped her legs around him as he lay over her, bracing himself against the headboard with an arm over his head.

"Take me, Peter," she pleaded.

With both of their energy spent, Peter lay down beside her. Dixie curled up beside him, and he put an arm around her.

"I love you so much," he said, pressing a kiss to her forehead.

Dixie leaned over him on an elbow and grinned down.

"Joshua and I bet on which of us would say that first," she said, smiling cheekily. "I bet against you. Guess I owe the brat a twenty now."

Peter gave a hearty laugh at the thought of the two of them betting over that.

"Best twenty dollars I ever spent," she said, leaning down to kiss him softly.

The End?

"Aunt Dixie, you look pretty!" Elliot exclaimed.

Dixie was brushing her hair in front of the mirror. She blushed slightly at the knowing look that Sarah gave her.

"I'm just going for a parole meeting, Elly," she said.

"What's a parole meeting?" Elliot asked.

"She's going to meet with Officer Peter," Sarah explained. "Remember him?"

Elliot nodded. "Is he your boyfriend, Aunt Dixie?"

"No!" Dixie replied, blushing harder.

"They're going on a date, though," Sarah said.

"No, we're not," Dixie corrected her.

"Oh, sorry, a 'parole meeting,' right?" Sarah asked, making air quotes around the words.

"I'm going to be late," Dixie mumbled. She grabbed her bag and the keys and headed out. It had been a week since Joshua had been released from the hospital, and she and Peter had shared that kiss. Dixie tried to push down the worry she felt, but they hadn't really talked since that day. He had missed their last parole meeting but suggested that they reschedule. When he suggested that they meet at a small diner that wasn't too far from her place, her hopes had risen again.

She was a jumbled mess of anticipation and nerves as she drove to the diner. She was a few minutes late, but she was surprised to see that Peter wasn't there when she arrived. She texted him as she got into a booth.

Hey, I'm at the diner. Are we still meeting?

It took a few minutes, but his reply eventually came.

I'm sorry I don't want to cancel again, we need to talk.

Dixie felt dread creep down her back. No one ever wanted to hear or see the words 'we need to talk' from the person they liked.

What about? She texted back.

We should do it in person. Do you think you could come over?

To your place? She asked, confused.

Yes.

His next message was an address.

Dixie sighed and got to her feet. She couldn't believe she was about to drive herself to go get dumped.

*

Peter's palms were sweating with nerves as he went to see the chief of the department. Thompson was known to be a hard-ass, but she had a soft spot for family. He had practiced his words countless times, so he knew he was prepared.

Her door opened, and he stepped in.

"What do you need, Mullaney?" she asked.

"I wanted to ask if I could be removed from parole duty," he said.

She looked up from the documents that she was holding. "Why?" she asked. "Parolee giving you problems?"

"No, nothing like that," he shook his head. "I just. My son just got out of the hospital. And I wanted to spend more time with him since I'm not back on active duty yet. I thought this would be the best opportunity."

Thompson looked at him with a scrutinizing gaze. "You sure about that, Mullaney?" she asked. "You're the one who asked to be put on parole."

"Yeah, I know," he said. "I just don't want to lose this opportunity to spend time with my son."

She gave him that scrutinizing look again before finally looking down. "Fine," she said. "You have a month. When you return, you're back on active duty."

"Thank you, chief," he said, sagging in relief.

"Yeah, yeah," she said, waving a hand at him. "Just make the most of it."

"Yes, ma'am," he said. He was already texting Dixie as he walked out of Thompson's office. He was going to get the girl. He drove home as fast as he could without breaking the speed limit. Dixie hadn't arrived by the time he got home, so he took a quick shower and ordered some food. When he heard a knock on the door, he knew it was her.

"Before you say anything, I just want you to know that you don't get to break up with me before we even started dating, okay?" Dixie barged in before he could say a word. "So, if you have some big break-up speech planned, you can save it."

She crossed her arms and glared at him, but he could see the vulnerability in her eyes.

"You think I asked you over here to dump you?" he asked, feeling a small grin begin to grow on his face.

"Why else would you say 'we need to talk'?" she asked.

"Maybe because I actually wanted to talk to you?" he said with a 'duh' tone.

"Talk, then," she challenged.

He couldn't hold the smile back now. "You are the most stubborn woman I know," he said, walking up to her. "You annoy the hell out of me, and you don't think before you act. You're brave and brash and so overwhelming sometimes."

"Kinda hard to tell if you're insulting or complimenting me, officer," she mumbled.

He stopped in front of her and held her face in his hands. "I'm in love with you, Dixie. I talked to my chief. I don't want to be your parole officer anymore. I want to be with you." Dixie looked up at him in disbelief. "Oh, now you're quiet?" he asked with a laugh.

She launched herself into his arms, sealing their lips together. If their first kiss had been a fire, this one was an inferno. They grabbed at each other's clothes as they stumbled across the room.

"Bedroom," Dixie panted against Peter's lips. "Please, Peter."

Peter nodded and led them to the bedroom without separating their lips. They crashed through the room and tumbled onto the bed together, giggling into each other's mouths.

"I'm in love with you too," Dixie whispered against his lips. "I want to be with you too."

Peter leaned down with a growl and took her lips again. His hands pushed her dress down her body, as Dixie nearly ripped his clothes off. When they were fully naked, she wrapped her legs around him as he lay over her, bracing himself against the headboard with an arm over his head.

He ground himself against her thigh, and Dixie moaned as he leaned down to cover her neck with love bites. She raised her hips, seeking friction against her hot entrance, and Peter leaned back to look her in the eyes.

"Do you want…"

"Yes, Peter, please," she panted out. He nodded and leaned up so he could rest on his knees. She let her legs fall open, and Peter took in the view of her naked body. Her full breasts rose and fell with each breath she took, and he could see her wetness, even from this distance.

"Take me, Peter," she pleaded.

He nodded again and took himself in his hand. He guided his hard dick to her entrance and pushed in slowly, drawing a loud moan out of Dixie. She wrapped her legs around his waist again, pulling him in deeper, and he grunted as he lost his balance for a second. Her walls squeezed him tight, and he leaned down to seal their lips as they rocked together slowly. After giving themselves some time to get a feel for each other and enjoy the rhythm, he pulled back again and grabbed her thighs.

He plowed into her with short fast strokes, pushing them both to the edge at an alarming speed.

"Peter!" Dixie cried out as she got closer to the edge. She screamed his name and more unintelligible words as she crashed over the edge. The sensations of her walls clenching and unclenching around him were enough to send Peter over the edge as well.

He came with a loud grunt, emptying himself inside her, after a moment he pulled out slowly and lay down beside her. Dixie curled up beside him, and he put an arm around her.

"I love you so much," he said, pressing a kiss to her forehead.

Dixie leaned over him on an elbow and grinned down.

"Joshua and I bet on which of us would say that first," she said, smiling cheekily. "I bet against you. Guess I owe the brat a twenty now."

Peter gave a hearty laugh at the thought of the two of them betting over that.

"Best twenty dollars I ever spent," she said, leaning down to kiss him softly.

Did you enjoy this book?

If so, please leave a review on Amazon!

Ready for more? Follow this and other favorites below!

https://www.ttpublishinghouse.com/legendsreborn

https://www.ttpublishinghouse.com/7wishes

https://www.ttpublishinghouse.com/mallcadet